Can I Bring Woolly to the Library, Ms. Reeder?

Lois G. Grambling • Illustrated by Judy Love

Charlesbridge

To all the Gramblings, librarian Linda Thompson,
second-grade teachers Barbara Coker and
Elaine Brownd, the Springlake-Earth school's
second-grade class, and to Randi, too.

—L. G. G.

To my niece, Dorrie, student of children's literature and
library science and lifelong bibliophile. Your insightful
enthusiasm rescued me from my creative doldrums. Thank you.

And to Jo Ellen Wright and Sandy Sonnichsen, librarians of the
Shedd Free Library, a quintessential, small-town library in Washington,
NH, for your gracious welcome and excitement about this project.

And to librarians everywhere for the encouragement you give our children
to discover the joy and exhilaration of reading that is paramount to their
intellectual and creative development. You are the guardians of our future.

—J. L.

Published by Charlesbridge
85 Main Street
Watertown, MA 02472
(617) 926-0329
www.charlesbridge.com

Library of Congress Cataloging-in-Publication Data
Grambling, Lois G.
    Can I bring Woolly to the library, Ms. Reeder? / Lois G. Grambling ;
illustrated by Judy Love.
        p. cm.
    Summary: Will a child's woolly mammoth create havoc if he is allowed in the library?
    ISBN 978-1-58089-281-0 (reinforced for library use)
    ISBN 978-1-58089-282-7 (softcover)
[1. Woolly mammoth—Fiction. 2. Libraries—Fiction.] I. Love, Judith DuFour, ill. II. Title.
PZ7.G7655Cak 2012
[E]—dc22   2011000652

Printed in Singapore
(hc) 10 9 8 7 6 5 4 3 2 1
(sc) 10 9 8 7 6 5 4 3 2 1

Illustrations done on Arches watercolor paper with transparent dyes
Display type and text type set in Big Limbo and Tempus Sans
Color separations by KHL Chroma Graphics, Singapore
Printed and bound in September 2011 by Imago in Singapore
Production supervision by Brian G. Walker
Designed by Diane M. Earley

If I brought Woolly to the library,
he could finally get a library card.
He could practice writing with Mr. Penn—
you know, the new library volunteer?

Sometimes Woolly mixes up his letters
or makes them backward,
but with more practice he could print his name
on your library card application.
And you could READ it!

With his library card
Woolly'd charge into the kids' section
and pick out a mammoth-sized
stack of books to read.

And he'd be so-o-o-o happy,
he'd let loose a long,
LOUD
BELLOW!
Maybe that would be a
good time
for Woolly and me to go over
the library rules.

Can I bring Woolly
to the library, Ms. Reeder?

Can I?

PLEASE?!

If I brought Woolly to the library
and that
THUMPING
noise
he makes when he walks
('cause he weighs a ton)
was too loud . . .

I could buy Woolly a pair of
extra-large,
fuzzy slippers.
That way
he'd be as quiet as a butterfly
landing on a buttercup . . .

NO
THUMPING

IN THE LIBRARY
Thank You!
—the Library St

and maybe I could pick up slippers
for those rowdy Bopsie twins, too.

Can I bring Woolly to the library, Ms. Reeder?

Can I?

PLEASE?!

If I brought Woolly to the library
and the returned books were piling up
on your "To Be Shelved" cart,
Woolly could shelve them for you.
He knows his numbers and ABCs.
And he can reach the tall shelves
with no problem.

Can you imagine if he got STUCK between the shelves!
We could get him unstuck.
BUT WHAT A MESS!

Maybe we should leave the shelving to you, Ms. Reeder.
But Woolly *could* sit at your desk
to check books in and out.
Then things would be back to normal . . .

almost.

Can I bring Woolly to the library, Ms. Reeder?

Can I?

PLEASE?!

If I brought Woolly to the library
and Cuddly Teddy wasn't in the Reading Corner
'cause several of his seams had split open
(probably from all the hugs he gets)
and he was in the toy shop being repaired,
Woolly could take his place.
(Woolly is very cuddly.)

Open your mind...
Open a Book!

Then the little kids
would still have plenty of places to sit
and someone who'd listen to them read aloud.
Woolly loves listening to little kids read.
Ms. Page in Literacy Services
says being read to
will help Woolly with *his* reading, too.

Can I bring Woolly to the library, Ms. Reeder?

Can I?

PLEASE?!

If I brought Woolly
to the library on Halloween
for your annual Storybook Character
Costume Party, we'd be a hit!
I'd go as the Big Bad Wolf.
And Woolly'd go as Little Red Woolly Hood.

Then you'd read us
SPOOKY stories.
We'd all listen
(Woolly, too),
bug-eyed,
terrified,
and

FROZEN WITH FEAR!

It'd be the coolest Story Hour ever!

Can I bring Woolly to the library, Ms. Reeder?

Can I?

PLEASE?!

If I brought Woolly to the library
and Mayor Pinchpenny came in with overdue books
(which he usually does)
and he complained

LOUDLY

that he wasn't going to pay any fines
'cause he'd renewed his books by phone last week
(but he hadn't),
Woolly'd flip Mayor Pinchpenny upside down
and shake him
(gently, of course)
until enough coins
had fallen from his pockets
to pay his fine.
Then Woolly would flip
Mayor Pinchpenny
right side up
and continue reading his book.

Can I bring Woolly
to the library, Ms. Reeder?

Can I? PLEASE?!

If I brought Woolly to the library
and it was your turn
to drive the bookmobile to Littletown,
and you were worried about driving
in the snow,
Woolly could get you there safe and sound.
(Woolly grew up at the North Pole
and doesn't worry about snow.)
But . . .

if you did slide into a snowbank,
Woolly'd just hook his curvy tusks
around the bookmobile's bumper
and P–U–L–L.
You'd be back on the highway
quick as a blink.

And if you had to spend the night
in the bookmobile,
you'd get used to Woolly's snoring.

Uh-oh, Ms. Reeder.
My mom's worried
that if Woolly came to stay with us,
he would get homesick—
like I did at camp last summer.
Being so far from his home
at the North Pole,
he would miss his parents a lot.
And the snowy, frozen weather, too.
So Woolly won't be coming to the library.
But he has a friend
who will be visiting family around here.
Woolly's friend loves to curl up
with a good book.
So . . .

Can I bring Saber
to the library, Ms. Reeder?

Can I?

PLEASE?!